We're good buddies!

Friend

Four amigos!

Great pals!

shape

by Amy Krouse Rosenthal and Tom Lichtenheld (friends)

Besties!

SCHOLASTIC PRESS • NEW YORK

What's so great about having
Friends?

We're glad you asked!

Friends

make you feel happy.

Friends

make you feel at home.

Friends

know how to make their own fun.

Friends...

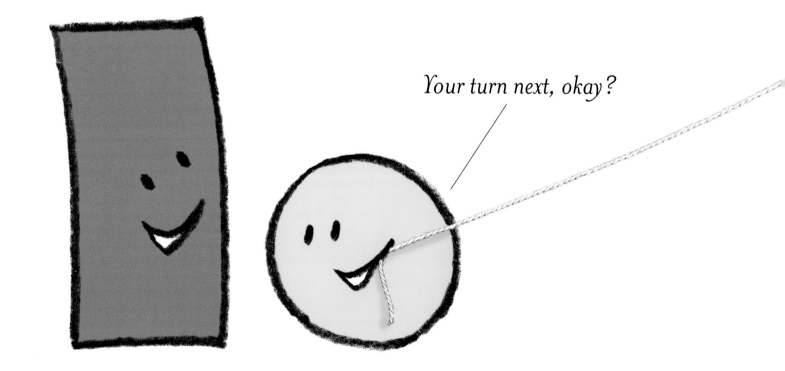

...play fair and

Friends sometimes

think the exact same thing
at the exact same time.

Friends

welcome others to join in.

So glad you could stop by!

Friends

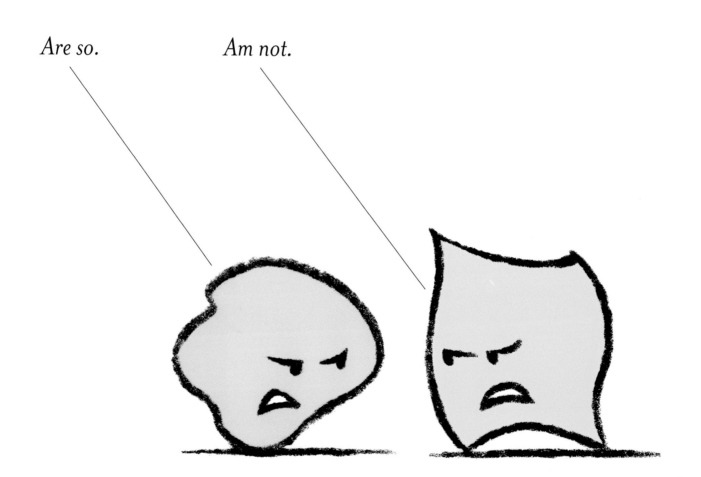

may quarrel...

Did so.   *Did not.*

...but they don't stay bent out of shape for long.

You know,
you have a good point.

Friends

will follow each other to the moon

and back.

Friends

stick together for
all of life's ups...

and downs.

Friends are always

there for you to lean on.

Thanks again for your support!

Friends are a gift,

**because they fill our lives
with joy and...**

friends to **the end**

 Published by Scholastic Press, an imprint of Scholastic Inc., *Publishers since 1920.* Library of Congress Control Number: 2013953391 ISBN 978-0-545-43682-3 10 9 8 7 6 5 4 3 2 1 15 16 17 18 19 Printed in Malaysia 108 First edition, September 2015 Typeset in Futura Book, Futura Bold, and Mrs. Eaves Italic. The illustrations were rendered in pencil with digital color. Book design by Tom Lichtenheld and Marijka Kostiw

Scholastic Press

(publishing house)

Amy dedicates this book to Jason.

Tom dedicates this book to Jan.

You dedicate this book to:

_____